Kirklees
METROPOLITAN · COUNCIL
CULTURAL SERVICES

Cultural Services Headquarters,
Red Doles Lane,
Huddersfield. West Yorks. HD2 1YF

**THIS BOOK SHOULD BE RETURNED ON OR BEFORE THE LATEST
DATE STAMPED BELOW. FINES ARE CHARGED FOR EACH WEEK
OR PART OF A WEEK BEYOND THIS DATE.**

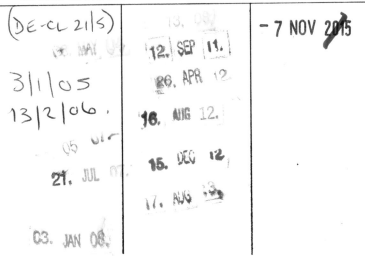

(DE-CL 21|5)

3|1|05
13|2|06

21. JUL

03. JAN 08.

13. 08

12. SEP 11.

26. APR 12

16. AUG 12.

15. DEC 12

17. AUG

− 7 NOV 2015

DÉ

DEWSBURY LIBRARY
01924 325080

You may renew this loan for a further period by post, telephone
or personal visit, provided that the book is not required by
another reader. Please quote the nine digit number on your
library ticket, and the date due for return.

W72   NO MORE THAN THREE RENEWALS ARE PERMITTED

Illustrated on

D1362595

550 438 198

KIRKLEES CULTURAL SERVICES	
55O 438 198	
Askews	13 MAY 2002
	£4.50
DE	CuL 26

You do not need to read this page -
just get on with the book!

First published in Great Britain by Barrington Stoke Ltd
10 Belford Terrace, Edinburgh EH4 3DQ
Copyright © 2002 Jeremy Strong
Illustrations © Scoular Anderson
The moral right of the author has been asserted in
accordance with the Copyright, Designs and
Patents Act 1988
ISBN 1-84299-052-7
Printed by Polestar AUP Aberdeen Ltd

Meet The Author - Jeremy Strong

What is your favourite animal?
A cat
What is your favourite boy's name?
Magnus Pinchbottom
What is your favourite girl's name?
Wobbly Wendy
What is your favourite food?
Chicken Kiev (I love garlic)
What is your favourite music?
Soft
What is your favourite hobby?
Sleeping

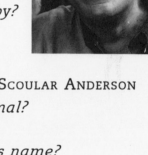

Meet The Illustrator - Scoular Anderson

What is your favourite animal?
Humorous dogs
What is your favourite boy's name?
Orlando
What is your favourite girl's name?
Esmerelda
What is your favourite food?
Garlicky, tomatoey pasta
What is your favourite music?
Big orchestras
What is your favourite hobby?
Long walks

This is for my friends in Athens:
Beth and Paris, Lydia, Phoebe and
of course, Iris (who is *not* an ostrich)

Contents

1 Who is KJ?   1

2 Mad Iris   13

3 Mad Iris Starts School   21

4 Anyone Want An Ostrich For Dinner?   31

5 Trouble In The Toilets   39

6 Katie Gets Stuck   47

7 An Unexpected Surprise   55

8 Ross Makes Up His Mind   63

Chapter 1
Who is KJ?

The note in Ross's bag was short and simple.

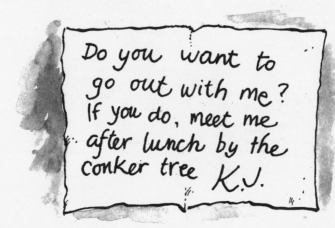

Do you want to
go out with me?
If you do, meet me
after lunch by the
conker tree K.J.

1

Ross turned a deep red and quickly folded the note. He pushed it to the bottom of his bag. He didn't dare look up, so he stared at his book. His mind was racing. KJ? That was the new girl – Kelly Jessup.

Kelly Jessup! Did Ross want to go out with *her?* Yes! Yes! Kelly made his legs turn to jelly. Kelly made his heart thump like a pounding drum. Kelly made ...

"Ross? Ross? Are you listening?" sighed his teacher Mrs Norton. "I said, what do you call a triangle with three equal sides?"

"Kelly," Ross replied dreamily.

"Don't be so stupid. You can't call a triangle *Kelly*," snapped Mrs Norton.

The rest of the class were laughing, all except for Katie. She waved her arm in the air.

"I think it's a great idea," she said brightly. "We could give every shape a name. Squares could be called Norman, and circles could be called Tracy, and rectangles ..."

"Do stop being silly," grumbled Mrs Norton, while the rest of the class gazed at her as if she were truly weird.

"Roger," Katie went on. "Roger Rectangle. That would be a good name."

"Oh, give me strength!" groaned Mrs Norton. "A triangle with three equal sides is called ..." But her voice was drowned by the bell for lunch.

Books were slammed back into desks or pushed into bags. Everyone made for the door.

Ross could hardly wait. Kelly Jessup – she was going to wait for him by the conker tree!

Ross bolted down his food and then sat on his chair in the hall, fretting. The dinner ladies wouldn't let him go until everyone had finished. Ross reckoned he would die of old age before that snail Gloria chomped her way through her rice pudding. At last she sucked down her last spoonful.

Ross dashed out to the playground but stopped before he got too close. "Play it cool," he told himself. "Take it easy. Just walk across slowly."

The conker tree came into view. Yes, Kelly really was there! She was laughing at something Ian Tufnell was telling her.

Ross snorted. Ian was an idiot. Okay, so maybe he was tall and good-looking and

brilliant at judo. Apart from that, he was a no-brain. Everyone knew that.

Ross drifted across and smiled at Kelly. She gave him a little frown. Ross raised his eyebrows at her several times.

"Is there something wrong with your eyebrows?" she asked.

"Yes! No! I mean the answer is yes!" grinned Ross.

"There *is* something wrong with your eyebrows?"

"No, not my eyebrows. The note. Yes is the answer to the note." Ross flashed his number one best smile.

All at once Ian was looming over Ross, who noticed what big hands Ian had. "Why don't you go somewhere else?" growled the judo expert.

But Ross didn't care about Ian. He was there for Kelly. He tried to look at her over Ian's broad shoulder.

"I do want to go out with you!" he shouted.

Ian's face turned to thunder. "You want to go out with *me*!"

Ross's heart sank. Why was Ian so stupid? "Not you – her! Kelly."

And that was when Ross's wonderful world turned into a hopeless pile of rubbish.

Kelly's eyes grew wide with horror. "Go out with you? You must be joking. I wouldn't go out with you if we were the last two people left on this planet."

Ian pushed Ross backwards. "Get lost, little boy. She's going out with me."

Ross's heart was shredded. It had been such a wonderful dream. He turned away, while Kelly and Ian sniggered at him.

A hand gently touched his arm and he looked up. It was Katie. She gave him a little smile.

"It's not that bad," she told him.

"It is," muttered Ross.

"The note wasn't from Kelly," she went on. "I didn't realise we had the same initials. KJ. It was from me."

"You!"

Katie smiled again, hopefully. "I put it in your bag after assembly this morning. What do you think?"

Ross was furious. He could not believe that he had got Kelly Jessup mixed up with Katie Jacobs. For heaven's sake – Katie Jacobs! The girl had freckles coming out of her ears! AND she was weird.

Ross turned on her. He was going to tell her that he wouldn't go out with her if they were the last two people left on the planet.

But he didn't. Instead his jaw dropped and he stared in stunned silence.

An ostrich had just come crashing through the school hedge.

An OSTRICH ????? !

Now the giant bird was striding across the playground. It was making straight for Katie and Ross, and it had a nasty glint in its eyes.

Chapter 2
Mad Iris

Ostriches are big birds, very big. When they are running straight at you they look even bigger. This one was like a huge black-and-white steam train, with feathers on all sides.

The children in the playground scattered in every direction. Mrs Norton, who was on playground duty, dived head first into a bush.

She was not the only one. Kelly Jessup and Ian Tufnell were already in there.

While everyone else was screaming and running away, Katie grabbed Ross and hissed at him. "Stand quite still!"

So Ross did as he was told. He couldn't have run away even if he wanted to. (Which he did.) His legs had turned to jelly.

The ostrich stopped short, just one stride away from where the two children stood rooted to the spot. It fluttered its very long eyelashes and studied them carefully.

What strange birds they were! They had feathers but they couldn't fly. Their knees were big and knobbly. They had the most odd-looking faces.

The ostrich stretched her neck forward and gently touched Ross's nose with her beak. He twitched.

"Hello," Katie said quietly. "I like you."

"Don't be stupid!" muttered Ross. "You can't *like* an ostrich."

"Sssh," Katie went on, in the same soft voice. "Just speak to her nicely. Don't move suddenly. Do everything slowly."

Katie reached into her bag as she spoke. She pulled out a chocolate bar. She was going to unwrap it, but the ostrich snatched it from her hand and ate it just as it was.

Then the bird stuck her whole head into Katie's bag. It ate her ruler, her felt tip pens and a spare pair of socks she had brought for PE.

"Oh!" said Katie.

"Ha, ha," laughed Ross, too loudly.
The ostrich lifted her head, looked at Ross
for a second and bit his ear. "Ow!" he yelled.

"Serves you right," said Katie, gently
stroking the bird's bony head. "You're a
clever ostrich, aren't you? Oh yes, and you
are so beautiful. I shall call you Iris."

Ross almost choked. "You *can't* call her
Iris! You're mad. *She's* mad!"

"Then I shall call her Mad Iris," smiled
Katie, and it seemed a very good name for
an ostrich.

Mrs Norton climbed out of her bush and
grabbed a big broom. She began to creep up
on the ostrich from behind.

"Come away from that bird," she told
Katie and Ross.

"She's not dangerous," Katie pointed out, stroking Mad Iris's long neck. The ostrich closed her eyes. She loved it.

But Mrs Norton knew a lot better. Ostriches *were* dangerous. She had to get rid of it. She didn't want an ostrich in the school playground. She waved her broom.

"Shoo!" she shouted.

Mad Iris jerked her head up.

"You're scaring her," Katie warned.

"Shoo!" yelled Mrs Norton, and she waved her broom again.

Mad Iris took a step towards the teacher. Her head suddenly shot forward and she pulled the broom from Mrs Norton's hands. She tossed it on the ground, and with one mighty kick, she broke it in half and tossed it to the side.

Mrs Norton couldn't speak.

Mad Iris took another step towards her.
What *was* that large, pink thing in the
middle of her face? Mad Iris reached
forward, grabbed Mrs Norton's nose in her
beak and tried to yank it off.

"Ow! My dose! Let go of my dose!" yelled
Mrs Norton, unable to breathe. She waved
her arms and jumped up and down.

At last Mad Iris let go, and the teacher
sank to the ground. The ostrich stepped
over the poor woman and strutted into the
school.

Chapter 3
Mad Iris Starts School

"Come on," said Katie. "We'd better follow her." She grabbed Ross by the arm and pulled him after her, much to his amazement.

By this time, Mad Iris was marching up and down the corridors, poking her long beak in everywhere. She pushed her way into the caretaker's little room and

snatched his sandwiches right out of his hands.

In the school office, she had a go on Mrs Perch's computer. Then she spread the neat piles of papers right around the office, so that she could see them more clearly.

While this was going on, Mrs Perch tried to hide in her big cupboard.

In the end, the ostrich went and stood in the headteacher's office. Mr Grimble didn't even look up from his desk. He just muttered, "What do you want, boy?"

Mad Iris picked up the phone and tried to swallow it. That was when Mr Grimble raised his head and found himself gazing at an ostrich. The ostrich gazed back at him and fluttered her long eyelashes. Mad Iris spat out the phone, in several bits.

"Oh," said Mr Grimble with care.
He moved slowly across to the window.
He opened it softly, while Mad Iris watched
him with a beady eye.

Then the headteacher jumped out and
ran off. Mad Iris emptied Mr Grimble's
filing cabinet and then went off to find
Katie. The ostrich liked Katie. She had
chocolate in her bag.

When Mr Grimble jumped out of the
window, Katie decided Mad Iris was going
to be great fun.

The ostrich followed Katie into her
classroom. All the other children ducked
behind the tables.

"We're going to keep her," Katie told
them all, and she turned to Ross. "Aren't
we?"

"Yes. We are." Ross couldn't believe what he was saying. Why was he agreeing with Katie Jacobs? She was mad! He didn't even like her!

"You can't keep an ostrich in school," sneered Kelly Jessup from behind Ian Tufnell.

"You've got twigs in your hair," Katie said coolly. Ross felt himself smile.

Then Ian Tufnell surprised Ross by saying that he thought keeping an ostrich in school would be a terrific idea.

And Kelly Jessup surprised Ian by hitting him. "It's a stupid idea," Kelly snarled. "Katie's just weird. Anyhow, the teachers will never let you keep her. I bet they are on the telephone to the police right now."

STAFF

And she was right. By this time, the teachers, including Mr Grimble, had locked themselves in the staffroom.

"It's as tall as Big Ben!" Mr Grimble shouted down the phone.

"It's got eight legs!" cried the caretaker.

"And six beaks!" squeaked Mrs Norton, who still had a very sore nose.

Mr Grimble put down the phone and turned to his staff. "It's all right," he said. "The police know all about that bird. It escaped from an ostrich farm. The keepers are on their way to the school right now. We shall soon get rid of it. Well then, who's for coffee? Any biscuits left?"

Outside the staffroom door, Ross's friend Buster listened at the keyhole. They were going to get rid of their ostrich! He hurried back and passed on the news.

"We've got to save her. What shall we do?"

"We should hide her," said Gloria. "We must find somewhere that nobody will ever think of. It will have to be somewhere big enough to put an ostrich."

There was a deep silence. It was only broken by Mad Iris, who chose this moment to make a long and rather rude noise, before making a mess on the floor.

"Urrgh! That's revolting!" cried Ian.

"She doesn't know any better," said Katie.

Mad Iris seemed to agree with her because she now tried to eat Katie's hair.

"GET OFF!" Katie slapped the bird's head and Mad Iris began to eat Mrs Norton's felt tip pens instead. Then she went back to

Katie's hair, only her beak was full of felt tips. She left squiggly, coloured marks all over Katie's head. "Stop it, you idiot!"

"I know what!" cried Ross. "We could put her in the toilet, and then it won't matter if she does a poo."

"You can't put an ostrich in a toilet," sneered Kelly. "She won't fit."

Ross turned very red. "I don't mean *in* the toilet *itself* – in one of the booths. I bet nobody will think to look there. You'd never expect to find an ostrich in the boys' toilets, would you?"

"He's right, you know," grinned Katie. "Well done, Ross – not just a pretty face!"

Ross gave her a big grin.

"Ooooooooooh!" went the class, while Ross turned even redder.

Chapter 4

Anyone Want An Ostrich For Dinner?

Mad Iris thought the toilets were very interesting.

First of all, she pulled the toilet roll off the holder and unrolled it. Then she wrapped the paper round the water tank, round the pipes, round the bowl, round Ross's head, and round Buster's legs.

Finally, she tossed the roll over the top of the open door. Everyone thought this was very funny, even Ross.

Mad Iris's next trick was to pull the toilet chain. Not only did the toilet flush, but the chain came off. Mad Iris swallowed it.

By this time, most people were falling about laughing. The best bit was when the bird got some loo paper stuck to her beak. When she groomed her feathers, it looked as if she was wiping herself.

Katie tried to be serious. She fixed Mad Iris with a stern gaze. "You've got to stay here and be very, very quiet. Do you understand?"

Mad Iris lifted one huge foot and plonked it in a toilet pan. Katie lifted it back out and wagged her finger. "Will you behave? You must keep quiet."

She had hardly finished when Buster came tearing down the corridor.

"There are some men coming!" he yelled. "Loads of them!"

From the far distance the children could hear the wail of sirens. It was getting louder. Then several police cars swept into the playground, followed by a fire engine. Did they think that the ostrich was going to set fire to the school?

Then a big, dark truck appeared. It slowed to a halt and several men in black leapt out. There was writing on the side of the truck.

"They've got guns!" whispered Ross. "They're going to kill our ostrich and turn her into dinner!"

They watched, white-faced, as Mr Grimble spoke to them. They could hear every word through the open windows.

"She escaped from our farm yesterday," one of the men declared.

"What are you going to do?" asked the headteacher.

"These stun-guns fire a drug that put her to sleep. After that, we'll take her back to the farm. She's going to be killed in the end anyhow. They all are. We send the ostrich meat to supermarkets all over the place. Tastes lovely!" One of the men grinned at Mr Grimble and smacked his lips.

Mr Grimble took a step back. He certainly did not want an ostrich in his school, but he was not at all happy about what was going to happen.

"We shall have to move the children out first. The staff can take the register in the playground to make sure that everyone is out of the building before you go in. And don't tell the children what you plan to do. It will only upset them."

But it was too late. The children knew, and they were already upset.

"Now what do we do?" wailed Gloria. "If we're taken outside, there will be nobody to look after Mad Iris."

They stared at each other glumly. From the far end of the school came the sound of their teachers, calling for them.

One by one they went back to their classes, and still nobody had thought of a plan.

The children were lined up along the corridors and led outside. Soon the school was oddly silent and empty.

At least it was *almost* empty.

There was an ostrich in a toilet cubicle, plonking one foot in and out of a toilet pan.

And hiding in a cloakroom, with their feet showing beneath some coats, were Ross and Katie.

The men in black picked up their stun-guns and strode into the school.

Chapter 5
Trouble In The Toilets

Ross and Katie huddled together in silence. Ross could hear Katie breathing fast. He reached down, found her hand and squeezed it. She squeezed back, and didn't let go.

Ross shifted his feet and felt nervous. He didn't want to give Katie the wrong idea. On the other hand, he had no idea what the wrong idea was – or the right one, for that matter.

Here he was, standing under some coats, with a girl holding his hand and an ostrich stuck in a toilet cubicle. It was no wonder he felt muddled.

Katie pushed the coats apart and peered out. It seemed to be all clear, but they could hear loud voices some way off. It would not be long before the men in black headed their way.

There was a terrible banging from the toilet. Ross dashed across to see what was going on. Mad Iris had discovered how to put the toilet lid down. And up. And down. And up again. *Bang bang bang bang!*

"Stop it!" hissed Ross. "The men will hear you!"

Mad Iris stopped. She tried to eat the buttons on Katie's shirt. They wouldn't come off, so she had a go at Ross's ears instead. Ross threw up his arms to protect himself. "Ouch!"

Katie giggled.

"It hurt!" growled Ross angrily.

"There, there. Shall I kiss it better for you?"

"No! I've just had an ostrich pecking my ear. I'm not going to let you have a go at it too!"

The smile suddenly vanished from Katie's face.

"Sssh, listen! I think someone is coming this way."

Ross quietly closed the toilet door and went out into the corridor.

He instantly flung himself back inside. Someone *was* coming! A large, heavy man was marching down the corridor checking every room, one by one!

Ross dashed back to make sure the ostrich was well hidden. Her feet could just about be seen through the gap between the door and floor, but there was nothing he could do about that.

"Stay very, very still. Don't say a word," whispered Ross to Katie. "We're going to hide in the next door toilet, OK?"

Mad Iris watched these strange children carefully. Why did they keep whispering? Something was going on. She decided to wait and see what happened.

Ross and Katie slipped into the next door toilet booth. Ross put down the toilet lid softly and climbed on to it.

"They mustn't be able to see our feet," he whispered, and Katie climbed up after him. Katie chose that moment to get a fit of the giggles and she started spluttering into her hand.

"Now what?" demanded Ross.

"I was just wondering what Mr Grimble would say if he opened this door and found us standing here."

Ross rolled his eyes. How come he was stuck in the boys' toilets with this crazy girl? He pulled himself up so that he could see over the wall into the ostrich's cubicle. At least *she* was behaving herself for once. Good.

The man out in the corridor was a big burger man. He had a big, round chest. He had a big, round face sitting on a big, round neck, all of which came from eating lots of burgers. He had just eaten one for lunch. He burped loudly as he wandered down the passage, checking the rooms, with his stun-gun at the ready.

Big Burger Man was talking to himself. "Is there anyone in here?"

The children heard a door bang as it was flung open. "No-one in *that* room!"

"Oho ho, I can see you! Peek a boo! Is there anyone in here?" the man went on. "No-one in there either."

Bang went another door.

The door to the boys' toilets crashed open.

"Oh me, oh my, it's a tiddly room for tiddlers!" sniggered Big Burger Man. "I guess I'd better check the cubicles."

Ross held his breath and Katie shut her eyes. The door of the toilet at the far end was opened.

"Nope," muttered Big Burger Man.

The next door opened.

"No," said Big Burger Man.

He opened the third door and found himself eye-to-beak with an ostrich.

"Ha! Got you!" cried Big Burger Man, and made a grab for his gun.

Chapter 6
Katie Gets Stuck

That was when Mad Iris decided to change the man's face a bit. She tried to pull off his nose and ears. That didn't work, so she tried to pull out his hair, and she was a lot more successful.

"Ow! Yow! You pesky chicken!" Big Burger Man staggered back, while Mad Iris banged the toilet lid several times to show how cross she was.

Big Burger Man took aim with his
stun-gun.

"Yeee-hah!" Ross flung himself over the
top of the door and landed on Big Burger
Man's shoulders. He clamped his hands over
the man's eyes.

Katie jumped up and down on the toilet seat. "Get him, Ross! Go on! Pull his head off!"

KRAK!

The plastic lid snapped in half and Katie's feet vanished into the bowl. A great spout of water jetted up over the sides. Katie couldn't move. Her feet were firmly wedged in the toilet pan.

Big Burger Man clawed at Ross with one hand, but Ross held on for dear life. Mad Iris joined in and began pecking at the man's clothes. Several rips appeared. Big Burger Man was staggering round, with Ross still on his back. He stumbled out into the corridor.

"GET OFF! You horrible baboon!"

At last he dropped his gun on the floor, pulled Ross from his shoulders and hurled him to the floor.

"Now I'll get that bird!" hissed Big Burger Man. "Where's my gun?"

Mad Iris had it. The ostrich liked big, shiny things. She kicked the gun around with her feet. She pecked it with her beak. And that was when it went off. *Bing!*

A little stun-dart shot out and stuck in Big Burger Man's ankle.

"You ...!" was all he could manage before he slumped to the ground.

Ross struggled to his feet. "Come on, Katie, we can't stay here. The others must have heard us by now. We'll hide upstairs."

Katie's face was white. "I can't move," she said. "My feet are stuck. Take Mad Iris

and go before the others get here. I'll be OK.
Go on, go, go, GO!"

Ross stared at her for a second and then
nodded. He pulled Mad Iris out into the
corridor and dashed up the steps.

She lolloped after him. Somehow the
ostrich sensed that Ross was on her side.
In fact, Ross was probably her only hope
now.

Ross searched wildly for a hiding place.
He heard footsteps and voices below. The
only door they could go through now led on
to the school's flat roof. Nobody, not even
Mr Grimble, was allowed onto that roof.
It was far too dangerous.

"There they are!" cried one of the men.
Ross began to panic. What could he do now?
Mad Iris gazed all around. What was that
big, red, shiny thing on the wall? It looked
tasty! Mad Iris pecked it. Hard.

Clang-a-lang-a-lang-a-lang!!

Alarms clattered. Water showered madly down from the ceiling. Mad Iris had set off the fire alarm and water sprinklers.

The men in black backed off for a moment, as water soaked through their clothes. Ross seized his chance. He opened the door onto the flat roof and pushed the ostrich through. Then he shut it behind him.

They stood on a big, flat, empty space. There was nowhere else to hide and nowhere else to go. They were all alone on top of the school, with the wind whistling in Ross's ears. He peered over the edge. The other children seemed miles away, like little matchstick people.

Ross stood on the roof with the ostrich, and he felt alone and helpless and afraid.

Then the door burst open and several
dripping men squelched out onto the roof.

"Game's over, boy! Don't move!" yelled
one.

Ross turned to the ostrich at his side.
"Fly!" he yelled. "Fly for your life!"

Chapter 7
An Unexpected Surprise

But of course, ostriches can't fly. Mad Iris was scared and she did what ostriches do when they are scared. She hid her head. She plunged her head down Ross's shirt.

The men took several steps closer.

"Just keep very still, boy," ordered one of the men. "That's a dangerous bird you've got next to you."

"She isn't dangerous!" cried Ross. "You've got guns, you're the ones who are dangerous."

"Don't be stupid now, just take one step this way, so we can get a good shot at the chicken."

"She's an ostrich," snapped Ross.
He twisted round so that he was standing between Mad Iris and the men.

"Are you always such a pain?" snapped one of them.

"You're a bigger pain than me," Ross replied.

"Wise guy, huh?" The men were getting cross. Ross knew this standoff couldn't last forever. Something would have to happen soon, and it did. The headteacher poked his head over the edge of the roof.

While everyone had been talking, the fire engine had raised its ladder. Mr Grimble had climbed up and now he clambered over the edge of the roof.

Ross sighed. The game was up. He would have to give in now. There was nothing more he could do.

The men in black grinned. "Thank you, Sir," said their leader. "If you could just remove the boy from our line of fire we'll deal with the chicken right away."

Mr Grimble stepped closer to Ross. He put a hand on his shoulder and gripped it hard. Ross's heart sank.

Mr Grimble eyed the five men. "We are not going to move anywhere yet," he said. "You can put down your guns and leave this building at once. I am in charge here and I want you off these school grounds in five minutes."

"But ..." began one of the men.

"No buts," insisted Mr Grimble. "The chicken, as you call it, will stay here with us."

"That ostrich is ours," cried the men.

"No, she isn't," smiled Mr Grimble. "I've just bought her for the school. We're going to keep her as our lucky mascot and we're going to look after her. Goodbye!"

The men backed off, muttering.

As they vanished from the roof, Ross realised that the whole school was cheering in the playground below. They were shouting and laughing and waving their arms, even Mrs Norton.

Mr Grimble, Ross and Mad Iris stood on the roof, together. Ross felt madly happy. Mad Iris just felt mad. She undid Mr Grimble's shoelaces.

"Behave yourself," snapped the headteacher. "If you don't I shall ... oh! She's eaten my glasses." Then Mr Grimble sighed. "I think it should have stopped raining indoors by now," he said. "Shall we go inside?"

Ross smiled. He thought that was a very good idea. They were halfway down the stairs when Ross suddenly remembered Katie. He wondered what Mr Grimble would say. Perhaps it would be better not to tell him? On the other hand, Ross couldn't just leave Katie in the boys' toilets.

"I think I'd better show you something," Ross said as they reached the toilets. Shouting came from inside.

"Ross! Are you out there? If you leave me here forever, I shall never hold hands with you again!"

Mr Grimble looked at Ross and his eyebrows slowly moved up his forehead.

Chapter 8
Ross Makes Up His Mind

"That sounds like a girl," he said, and Ross nodded glumly. "Why is there a girl in the boys' toilets?"

"I think you'd better take a look," Ross suggested, and Mr Grimble went in.

"Ross!" shouted Katie. "If you get me out you can kiss me if you want!"

Mr Grimble's eyebrows rose even higher. Ross went scarlet and gave a little shrug.

"Girls," he said. "What can you do?"

The headteacher pushed open the door. Katie still had both feet firmly stuck in the toilet pan. She gave Mr Grimble a pale smile. "Oh! I thought it was Ross."

"So it seems."

Katie hardly dared ask, but she had to know. "Did you hear what I just said?"

"About Ross and ...?" Mr Grimble broke off and shook his head. "Didn't hear a word," he said. "We'd better get you out, hadn't we?"

It took half an hour of struggling to free Katie's feet from the toilet pan. Mad Iris tried to help by pulling the chain several times. She wrapped Mr Grimble in toilet paper. Finally, when he lost his temper and shouted at her to stop, the ostrich plunged her head down the back of his jacket and hid.

At last, Katie was able to stand on dry ground. Her feet and ankles were a bit sore, but otherwise she was fine. They went out onto the playground, where they were greeted with huge cheers. Mad Iris strutted this way and that, looking very proud of herself, even though she hadn't done anything useful.

Kelly Jessup came over to Ross with a winning smile and laid a hand on his arm. "You were just *so* brave," she said. "And clever. You can go out with me if you want."

Ross looked across to where Katie Jacobs was talking to Mad Iris. Katie Jacobs! She had freckles coming out of her ears. Her face was covered with felt tip pen. She was friends with an ostrich. She was mad.

Ross smiled at Kelly. "I'm with her," he said. "And the ostrich."

Barrington Stoke was a famous and much-loved story-teller. He travelled from village to village carrying a lantern to light his way. He arrived as it grew dark and when the young boys and girls of the village saw the glow of his lantern, they hurried to the central meeting place. They were full of excitement and expectation, for his stories were always wonderful.

Then Barrington Stoke set down his lantern. In the flickering light the listeners were enthralled by his tales of adventure, horror and mystery. He knew exactly what they liked best and he loved telling a good story. And another. And then another. When the lantern burned low and dawn was nearly breaking, he slipped away. He was gone by morning, only to appear the next day in some other village to tell the next story.

Barrington Stoke would like to thank all its readers for commenting on the manuscript before publication and in particular:

Sade Akin
Christopher Allen
Jill Atkinson
Paul Bardsley
Mark Bardsley
Charlie Benson
Hannah Brown
Daisy Burgoyne
Rhodri Buttrick
Lawrence Chandler
Natalie Chandler
Louise Connet
Hilary Coupe
Josephine Cox
Wendy Garvie

Joe Gubba
Kristian Hampton
Luke Hampton
Katy Hampton
Andrea Hampton
Joshua Harvey
Lysander Hays
  Watson
Dean Hill
Laura Howe
Grace Kindred
Sue Kindred
Mandy Kirk
Robert Lawson
Leanne Leil

Lynn Linsell
Shannon Mais
Chloe Metcalfe
Deanne Myers
Maxine O' Brien
Dominic Phelps
Carl Smith
Lisa Stevens
Jonathan Stratford
Kelly Taylor
Jade Telfer
Alistair Tomlinson
Emma Williams

Barrington Stoke Club

Would you like to become a member of our club? Children who write to us with their views become members of our club and special advisors to the company. They also have the chance to act as editors on future manuscripts. Contact us at the address or website below – we'd love to hear from you!

Barrington Stoke, 10 Belford Terrace, Edinburgh EH4 3DQ
Tel: 0131 315 4933 Fax: 0131 315 4934
E-mail: info@barringtonstoke.co.uk
Website: www.barringtonstoke.co.uk

If you loved this story, why don't you read . . .

Living with Vampires

by Jeremy Strong

Are your parents normal? Kevin's parents are really odd. They can turn people into zombies. Blood is their favourite drink. Even worse, they are coming to the school disco! How can Kevin get his parents to behave normally so he can impress the beautiful Miranda?

You can order this book directly from:
Macmillan Distribution Ltd, Brunel Road, Houndmills,
Basingstoke, Hampshire RG21 6XS
Tel: 01256 302699